Poetry on FIRE

Asty

Author's Tranquility Press
COLLEGE PARK, GEORGIA

ASTY / Author's Tranquility Press
2300 Camp Creek Parkway Ste 120 #1255
College Park, GA 30337
www.authorstranquilitypress.com

Ordering Information:
Quantity sales. Special discounts are available on quantity purchases by corporations, associations, and others. For details, contact the "Special Sales Department" at the address above.

POETRY ON FIRE / ASTY
Hardback: 978-1-966088-61-5
Paperback: 978-1-966088-62-2
eBook: 978-1-966088-63-9

Contents

A bit of nothing

Among all I hold dear
This one is of my prime directive
"Doing nothing"

In my mind every day
I try for a while to go away
Taking time off
Where to be aloof

To be distant from the daily faux
And not thinking of tomorrow
Forget about yesterday's regrets
Get rid of the stress

Only interested in the present
Feel the beat of my existence
And not agonizing about what might have been
Just experiencing "la joie de vivre" as it is meant

As a result putting down the heavy load
Take pause
Setting aside the negative thoughts
And slowly regain strengths I have lost

Being on that meditative excursion
I can hear the pulse of creation
Be aware with all my senses
Back to the essence

My heart then will get insight
While my imagination roams through the sites
Reaching out to the beyond
As I listen to the silence

There… I found how a little bit of nothing can be everything
And that everything is not much of anything
If there is no time for process
No moment of recess

For life is really something else
And sometime more is actually less
As many things become unfeasible to us
When we try to hold the world like "Atlas"

My Accent

It is to say that my accent is no easy listening
Words have an abroad articulation in my uttering
Implode consonants pronounced in clatter
On a limited vocabulary create a language barrier

Foreign idioms get mixed in my statement
Influencing the outcome of the dialogue to be bent
Spoken into a jargon
Which sometimes challenged the folks who listened

The selective nouns do not always capture my perception
As I put more connotations to relate my opinions
Even when the syntax is organized in my mind
And the sequences grammatically well defined

At time it will express a slang meaning
As the tempo differs from my feelings
And unlike the sentiments I try to reason
My voice echoes a dissimilar interpretation

I will have low pitches that fluctuate
Acute and crave resonances that vibrate
Through my mouth comes out notes I cannot forsake
Noises in the background that is tough to shake

As the emphasis stressed the syllables
Elevated rhythms become unstable
While the adverbs are conveyed in inflections
With absent adjectives compromising the diction

More than often while I talk
The vowels in the vocal balked
Conjugating the verbs in an improper tense
Putting strain on a sentence

These derivations do not quite enunciate my level of education
However, accentuate that I am not native of this nation
With intonations that are particular to my parentage
The peculiarities in the phrases tie a line to my heritage

An accent as a phonic treasure
Is the lingo of an individual's ancestors
Sounds entrusted in his twist of tongue that is often
Due to the location of his culture's origin under the sun

An unusual recipe

Giving a good first impression
Might need a touch of elegance
Thus bring the traditional courtship
And do not forget about chivalry

A pinch of charm widely spread
With a little flirting well dispersed
Blended with a bit of humor
Will show excellent manner

Do not pound on the conversation
Nor whip the words for attention
Release your sentences in eloquence
With both of your interest as stimulation

To have her relish your persona
Mashed in three scoops of charisma
And a cup of sensitivity
Combined with a spoon of sincerity

Add to your sweet sensations
A dash of common sense
As you mélange the mild feelings
Let the seasoning thoughts stir

Get it to be a shimmering evening
Marinated in pleasant music
As the mix of romantic ambiance
Sauté down the tension

Evenly buttered up the moment
And gradually include your special ingredient
Before putting it to bake in the oven
As the body temperature rises to 90° Fahrenheit

Watch closely her glazed skin
The arousal of her puffed lips
The tasteful colors of her blushed cheeks
That boiled the blood and make you flip

This is of a secret family recipe
That must be concealed in the gens
Hidden emotions in the heart
That will spice the flavor of life

Beauty

I want to individualize pretty
Diversify beauty
Have it be the spirit of every debutante
To carry without an image consultant

I want to allow each creature their own identities
Away from the commercial ideas
And have them show the essence of their characters
Beyond the superficial features

As they learn to embrace their flaws
State their unique charms
They will get connection to the sole magnetism
The genuine source of their magnificence

Everyone with their natural appeal
Will bring something regal
Quality inherited from birth
Just as the lord intended

In the depth of their charisma
An exclusive taste of fashion in aura
For confidence as a trait in seduction
Can personalize the attraction

They would not be mimicking the style of the magazine idols
Nor clone the walkway models
Whose statues are highlighted by cosmetic artists
And pictures edited by Photoshop specialists

Each person will reach and touch the core of the human being
Bringing out the signature of heaven
On what the original portrait be
Of their own version of the goddess "Aphrodite"

The Believer

A man of religious faith can be fatal
Fidel to one call
He is the worst kind
Have the best in mind

To him the cause is just
In destiny he trusts
His existence is for the fight
His actions are not in doubts

He will take a stand
Have no concern for pain
This to him is preordained
So he throws aside all discontents

Strictly devoted to the quest
He is willing to put his conviction to the test
He is a formidable warrior
A dedicated soldier

He thinks of himself as but a tool
Chosen to achieve a greater good
His life as a fanatic
Is a path that is uncompromising

He is a weapon of fate
And always a threat
He is bold
Therefore could be lethal

His emotions are deep in the pits
And he is not a skeptic
May not be the instigator
But truly believes in the order

The Big Dog

Barking at the wrong trees
As part of the social niche
I went without a leash
Fetching up frisbees

Pretending to be the big dog
And being train to crawl
Stinking the rug
Toying with rubber dolls
Being on the long stand
Man's best friend

As push comes to shove
Playing ball
Answering when called
Got me nothing but puppy love

Like an itch I can't scratch
As member of the kennel club
What was to be a catch
Having that ticket stub
Had me hitting the trail
Chasing my own tail

Since old habits die hard
I will go sniffing for troubles
Digging holes
Trespassing on my neighbors' yards

Living with the title of fleabag
Certain this be just a little mishap
And though a missing pet with no tag
Thoughts I could take it as a catnap
Had me laid on my back
But nobody rubbing my stomach

Through my name being dragged in the mud
Still running after a bumper
Slobbering all over
I growled at the hot rods

Being cousin to the bloodhound
A breed whose senses were mild
Instinctively I can smell conceited around
The scent of foxiness in the wild
That come to arouse under the starry line
The pursue of the two-legged canines

Though joining the life in shantytown
My mind never got rescued from the pound
I enjoyed that hunting ground
With a fear of being tied down

Unable to be adopted as a companion
Eager for a bone to pick
Feeling trapped and abandoned
Chewing on a stick
I went in more spots than have a dalmatian
Searching for a fire hydrant to pee on

For to countless paths well-known
Among the many creatures I've tracked
The only one I found longer to take tack
Was my own

Cheap Art

Society has made living into a cheap art
Now you can love without a heart
The gilt frame of prenuptial agreements
Has made legalized affections a bargain

Exhibited on the open market
Individuals displaying as property chattels
Come exposing their acclaimed youthful features
Auctioning to the highest bidders

Too often handcrafted figures
With bodies embedded as pretty as a picture
Come advertising their grasping concepts
Painting the town red

As full-size silicon Barbies
Tantalizing the sugar daddies
In their search for the exclusive lifestyle
They are the fashions of the desperate wives

Quick to sell their souls to any wealthy buyers
These prospective gold diggers
Are to be mistresses of the elite households
The consortiums decorative molds

Having affairs with their own husbands
While married to "Benjamin Franklin"
They get prerogative to board the party bus
Memberships at the country clubs

As so imported to their main focus
To reinforce their benefactors status
They characterized the discounted pleasures
Attributing depreciation to significant others

For to have vended all self-respect
To be utilized as a sex object
Ascribed to them only the worth of an ornament
Like that of a "poupee de salon"

The Clock

As the clock revolves
I watched life evolve
Rotating seconds in instants unfolds
Digits on the dial move

Turning with the wheel of time
Marking the changes in a ticking rhyme
Running through the ages
Adding to the mileages

Pieces undeviating from their aims
Hand and hand remain
Connected by a single knob
Setting history in a log

Through the spacing among the numbers
Restless minutes rushed on the hour
Measuring the day all the way to the rim
Striking on the chime

The clock goes by the amount of sand dripping in the glass
The orbit of the earth circling the sun within the axis
Chronologically it arranges the months on the calendar table
Putting appointments on schedule

The grandfather clock more than swinging the pendulum
Makes man part of the continuum
Checking regularly life's pulses
Mending the heart

The Dandelion

Learning to wield
As a flower that breeds in the field
Acquainted with filth
The Dandelion doesn't need to be provided good tilth

Watered by tears shed from the "Heaven's"
Cultivating her own garden
Unlike the elegant rose nurtured in the lot
She does not blossom in a pot

Being of the wildlife
Drawn in the internal strife
She is nothing like the grouping at the florist store
Nor the house plant on the parlor near the door

Deep with the weeds
Like many seeds
The growth of her blossoming
Is best in spring

Though distant to the Fleur-de-Lis
She lays down with the moonlight bliss
To adorn a stage for the grasshopper at night
And tint in the twilight

Following the general gist
And budding in the morning mist
She bowed in reverence to the "Aquilon" blows
Dances while the "Zephyr" rows

To not having her own backyard
In the prairie standing guard
She has a beauty only nature can compare
In the soil no despair

She is the basic ornament of the "Earth" décor
Kind of difficult to ignore
She spread around in the wind
Making life colorful in the prairie

Debt to society

There is a toll for the times that I let slip by
A fine for being unkind
And levied on my existence
Are taxes for being sentient

There is a fee entering this world
A wage for being granted birth
A fare for breathing the air
And a tab for being unaware

For the wisdom of my ancestors
Are morals I have to sponsor
Undertake as my inheritance
With interest principles for the generation next

An amount of regrets has to be defrayed
For the lives I strayed
And to the heartaches I imposed
Retributions have to be made

A bail was set for my criminal offenses
At the expense of romance
And the low balance of my intimacy
Is to sum of my insecurity

I got billed for the lies I told
Charged for being a faux
And to the payments beholden
I am obliged to be alone

The price on my head
Is of the due dates I disregarded
And in the account of decency
I have lost all credit

Although benefits supposed to outlay cost
My case is a bust
And to my debt to society
I cannot declare bankruptcy

It is certain that my Owings
Do not all pertain to funding
And not much are recorded on paper
But still I have to pay the piper

DMV
(Dangerous Moving Vehicle)

Given the curvature in figure
This automaton has it engage a driver
Easily will gear shift his thoughts
Having him clutched his breath

Smoothly as he is being distracted
Maneuvered by body signals
She will plot a fender bender
A deliberate rear ender

As a designed attraction
In provocative fashion
This deadly contraption in moving violation
Seizes the attention

Although receiving many citations
She still flouts the regulations
And her illegitimate flirting on the rails
Has made her loving criminal

Her unlawful mode of "Stationary Park"
Does not restrict her from urban lots
But she has been warned for the reckless seduction
In the usage of this dangerous vehicle

She can surely veer your wheel
With her system of power steering
Force you to ignore the red lights
Driving you wild

In the way her engine routs the crowd
She is a liability for the roadside
Habitually a hazard to the public
For she brakes the flow of relationships in transit

This automobile is a threat to highway safety
Too often she has jeopardized the traffic
Has gotten many speed tickets
Made erotic chasing wicked

Statistic shows she has injured hearts
No matter how skilled and experienced were the operators
Always enthusiastic about the joyride
This vessel will crush your pride

Getting into her lane is but a taunting venture
The damages are measured by your fervor
Chances are you will crash and burn
Be left on the scene with a hit-and-run

Dope

I was dope
It is no wonder I got smoked
I was shit for brain
Told to be Psychoactive like hemp

Lost all my pride
As I was being bought on the street side
All the while I am being sanctioned as a medicine
Licensed to lessen extreme physical pain

Still I will get you high
Make you stupefy
For as a so-called prescription for cancer
It is hard coping with such malignant tumor

I am to get you stoned
Addicted to the bone
Not like the counter drugs
Just ask any pot-headed thug

Legally named "Marijuana"
Related to the family of "Cannabis sativa"
I often get buzzed about in the world of narcotics
As the infamous weed

So abused like tobacco plants
Feeling like a stinky joint
Becoming a member of the recreational substances
As reefer I blunt their senses

The dealers have no respect for me as a natural flower
Despite being butted by religious groups as a sacramental herb
And with my intent to be in big traffic case
They seldom distribute me as free base

Being the puffing piff at the bash
As ganja carried in a stash
Conveniently in a small bag
I get to be the usual drag

Later holding me on the fingertips
They burn me as dry leaves
While they crack jokes and laugh
That I am nothing but grass

Drinking Bud's

When the system is getting on your "Heineken"
You feel confused and forsaken
Heavier your stomach bellied down
While the room spins around

In a hubbub you are singing your drunken songs
Dots of colors spots your eyes
You start seeing double
But still you are hitting the bottle

As your head batters the ceiling
On the counter your back teeth are drowning
However you try to empty the pot
Attempts to strut

Dragging yourself to the lavatory
As you are drooling
Holding on the wall in a slippery slime
Can't even walk the line

You want to spout out the liquor
But it is as gushing out your liver
Something is obstructing your gullet
You begin to secrete sweat

Your skin takes on the complexion of a sallow
You think of drinking "Drano"
Jaws open your tongue repeatedly emerged
As an unusual turbulence in your gorge pursed

On your knees you go facing the toilet
Having a hard time closing your palette
Both hands hugging the latrine
You feel as falling into a ravine

Side of your cheeks against the stool bowl
Smelling the residues of previous bowels
There is no way of being instantly sober
The alcohol in your blood can not be filtered

The deeper is your groan
Further is your intoxication
You are past tipsy
Dancing like a gypsy

Better say your prayers
Do not be a drunken stupor
And go popping pills
So you can go steering the wheel

Just linger a bit longer
Pick up the phone and dial my number
No need to explain why
Simply call before the "DUI"

I will have you bailed
Prior to you getting jailed
Bring you home safely
And put you to sleep

Tomorrow might be ailing
With a constant discomforting buzzing
All in the story of a nasty hangover
But tonight let me be your designated driver

A dummy

Molded to the figure of a human being
I am to be a dummy
Somehow manipulated by wire
Stringed by the puppet master

A marionette made for slapsticks
Displaying life in travesty
I was brought on a routine performance
For a loutish exhibition

Limited to a box
I was well compacted
Always kept in the dark
A doll with a knack

They had me as a hand in a dirty sock
Before putting me in a ventriloquist act
And like the wooden boy
They throw my voice

Even with my "Pinocchio" nose
I could not smell their ruses
And with my feet dangling in the air
I could not be grounded

Sometimes dressed as a mannequin
I get to play the "harlequin"
Bringing joy to the spectators
Like the character of a court jester

In a world that is bigger than a suitcase
I as a man had to have my dreams folded
In brief be put in my place
To fit in this populace

Just like a "Bozo"
I went along with the show
Providing live entertainment
For the exclusive audience

If I was lucky
On the podium where I appeared
Society will toss me a buck or two
But never giving me the respect I am due

The Eviction

I was kicked out of a loving relationship
For my unworthy misdeeds
Did not realized how good I had it
Until she threw me in the street

Apologizing for my action
Hoping her broken heart will mend
I begged for leniency
A chance to redeem the intimacy

On my knees swallowing my pride
I asked to be forgiven for my lies
But already she had bottled
With her feeling shuttered

Like receiving an eviction
Losing all rights to her affection
I was no longer allowed a premise
For she crossed me off her lease

Having my spirit slumped
After being dumped
I left with her for safekeeping
All my personal belongings

She returned to me the hurtful statements
But held on my heartfelt possessions
Images of still nights
When passion glowed in the moonlight

I would be comfortable to be referred as a Cheat
Be some sort of nostalgia in her story
But I have yet to be mentioned as an ex
Cited as a used to be she rejected

Although I have found a place to hang my hat
She rented me apart
And the memories in my head
Still keep me a waif

Regaining that sense of home
Is hard when you cannot move on
There is no safe haven from these thoughts
No way to get rid of these spoils

My itinerant living does not get me far enough
No address is so distant to have me forget her touch
None of the regrets I hold can be lessened
Until time let me know it is sufficient

From the beginning

Eons ago man watched the night sparkled
He saw the glittering eyes of the gods
Gazed at the spirits of his ancestors

By constellations he sorted out the sky
Lay it down by clusters on a chart
Patterned it to glamorize his myth idols

Trusting in the alignment of those crystal lights
He wrote legends and fables of those
strange shimmers in the dark
Uses them as signs to justify aspects of
human behaviors with the horoscope

Astounded by those radiant rocks falling with flaming tails
He sang and danced celebrating their heavenly might
While he kneels in prayer to influence the nature of things

As visual aids in long journeys around the world
He utilized them as beacons
Their twinkling positions as reference for direction

He even draws on their configurations to create a language
That prophets employed in translating messages
for upcoming events
A method of study that astronomers points to in tracking
movements of planets in the zodiac

Often standing on top of the hills
With only a yearn to make truth of a dream
He reaches out to those blazing candles

In silent clause
Looking toward the celestial arch
He wishes up on those he named "Stars"

A Gamble

I was playing it safe
Not knowing how to take a chance
Did not want to roll the dice
Take a risk on life

Since I wanted to change my outcome
I had to get in a daring game
And put it big on the table
Take a gamble

The hand on the deal
Could change my fortune
But I always shake
When the stake is raised

To bet everything on living
Just to reach a dream
Maybe my lucky break
My only slake

No one has all the angles
But if I do not lay wager on my goal
I might as well fold
Be recalled back to the womb

Trying with high hope
And not void my card
Is the state of venturing
That will let me into the ante of winning

The Guide Book

Experience as a vantage point
Is a token of wisdom
Tutoring me that failures are not final
And mistakes are not carved on stones

Helps me understand the reason for humility
Explained in the book of living for dummies
Whispers to me who to lean on
And when to stand alone

It makes me wild yet civilized
Tells me how I should lose my disguise
And has I get to socialize
To keep an open mind

Always testing my ego
It gets me to confront my shadows
Lectures me on the tricks of the trade
By using data I accumulated

Informs me when to take hints
For every action has consequences
Taught me how to give esteem wonder
Therefore respect from others

It gives me skills to be proficient
With practice becoming instinct
As part of an inner voice acquired through ages
Like the teaching techniques habitual to the sages

It is now the "savoir faire" of my character
Originally written by my encounters
The style for my personality
Adding awareness to my integrity

Experience is neither good nor bad
Only what you obtain from the situation is right
The positive lessons are not easily grasped
Constructively hard to entrap

It puts my doubts aside
And lets me perceive beyond the sight
While calming my anger
Bringing hope to my despair

In giving me a particular perception of human being
A little bit about what is to be happy
It got me to trust my feelings
Find out what love means

This manual of my ventures
Abets me to be proud hearted as a blue collar
Making me to be knowledgeable
Following nature's principles

It is the gift I received
For the life I live
And everything becoming fate
In the choices I made

Heart attack

She came like a shock
More like a stroke
Never have I been so scared
About what I feel

It was hard catching my breath
Her sight almost had me choked to death
The blockage of reasoning in my head
Somehow resulted in stomachaches

This occlusion of my vital force
Must have damage my brain thoughts
And with a shortage of oxygen in my blood
I was falling in love

It was with no warning signs
That she strode my mind
Got me to that state of stimulus
On the brim of mental fatigue

Anxiety was diagnosed as my condition
As I was seeing her in slow motion
Something more of an erotic mode
During this unfamiliar episode

No more was I immune to infatuation
Now that I could die of passion
Just this cardiac arrest
Could have me end up in an incessant bliss

Although rehabilitation could alleviate the pain
And holistic healing could help as a medicine
There were no homeopathic remedy to this ill
No cure to this deadly malady

It is of a terminal ailment
Subjective to more than romantic treatments
It tend to require physical involvement
A mutual interaction till kingdom come

Compromising is to be of my well being
The intake of any healthy relationship
Never will I be the same
Vain taking life's moment

As it was confirmed of the live prognosis
The test return from the laboratory concluded
That all symptoms were in fact
The outcome of a heart attack

The immigrant

Being of a third world country
With no doubt got me screened
I was but a resident alien
Just an insignificant denizen

An immigrant embarked on a raft
Sailing a drifted path
Going against the waves
In a life with no compass

Praying for a fair wind
Rowing the unknown ocean
In the search of a familiar cluster of stars in alignment
A sign in the horizon

Afloat like a broken deck
Deported from the remain of a shipwreck
Baring a heavy load at a loose end
And slowly sinking to the bottom of oblivion

I was not going to wait to be salvaged
Nor let myself be submerged
So I roughed up English as a third language
To at least be average

Despite my permanent green card
I was just a visa
And although my "passport" got me through
It was not a "passé-partout"

I got stamped with a foreign label
Not belonging to the proper pigeonhole
And given a stigma
For not being born in "America"

This stereotype had flagged my beliefs
Seeing that even in the land of the free
The realm of "Lady Liberty"
Becoming a citizen does not naturally come with a welcoming

It seems that the forefathers' promise of equal rights
Has yet to be a reality in civil acts
For in the eyes of the law I am still divisible
Under this nation of "God"

In the zone

In the course of making love
I was zoned out
Here and there in intermediate dimension
Embodiment of two in unison

She was me as I was her Both spirits in singular
Heightened by her ecstasy
I was living the fantasy

From the inside out
Unaware of what was happening to the heart
I felt as coming out of the womb
Seeing love for the first time

I sensed her mind and my intertwining
No dichotomies between thoughts and actions
I was in the culmination of reality
Feeling every sensation in the body

Later finding out that what we do not know about love
Is far greater than what we do

Le Don d'un sourire
(The gift of a smile)

It doesn't cost a dime
But the benefit is sublime
Enriched the aspect of a character
Making him more receptive to humor

A smile with a release of endorphin
Will lighten the burden
Assuage fear in the brain
Facilitate the body to endure pain

No intent to burst a gut
It is a boost of joy that juts
Beyond the corner of the mouth
To hold even when things go south

A smile as an attractive feature
Is a force of nature
The indicated mentality
Of an affable personality

So, bring it to your social environment
And let it comfort the lament
Be that on the street
The upbeat for the down spirits

Though not always the antidote
It can on a positive note
Assist in managing mayhems
Strengthen the immune system

A smile doesn't have to show teeth
To be an uplift
What is in the world to be envisage
As a universal language

There none too soon
Let it in segment of your misfortunes
Be in reserve for all suffering
A remedy for healthier living

Down to its fine art
A smile is kindness to the serene heart
It will soothe the mood
Paint you with a new attitude

Truly smile
To make life worthwhile
Doesn't demand any skill
Nor any battle of wills

So, smile whenever you feel gray
To liven your day
It can raise the confidence
Sparks a romance

Always grin to stay sanguine
Let the pleasance reign
Spreads pass your lips
In the expressions you keep

So, if drifting like a lost soul
Someone is being resentful
And won't give you a smile
Don't keep the climate hostile

Be generous let the shine soars
Handover yours
For nobody is indeed of a smile endowed
Then the one who does not know how

Live theater

Just like a cheap show at the theater
Life can be meager
Too often the acting is so mediocre
That nobody gets the big picture

It is of the first time producer
And this unrenowned director
In a low budget expense
With extras working for a pittance

It is hard to stay in a role
That is not specified on a scroll
Difficult to understand a character
When you do not know his moral fiber

Even with plenty of space to improvise
Do something on a fly
Trying to cope with the unwritten lines
You somehow have to carry things out

Extemporizing on "Broadway"
Is to be your big break
But do not let go of your privacy
To get attention from the public

Make sure your interaction with the fans
Do not sway your judgment
And not allow slandering of your good name
Bring into disrepute your aim

Let respect as your agent
Have integrity to be your introduction
Do not let vanity as a representation
Be the image you portray in your audition

For with no previous rehearsal on being human
Confusion may be the nature of your sins
Because unlike a play edited before being performed on stage
Living is not of the script on a page

The Look

I have heard some savvy speakers
Read some breath-taking literatures
But none with the sudden impact
As the strike of an eye contact

A look can take a particular turn
Without a spoken word leaves you to burn
Though the deal not signed
Bearing a special effect on the mind

Expressed in a still communication
It can capture the attention
Silently could be the thing to say
Have outward the thoughts you are trying to convey

Unlike the blink of the wink
keeping you on the brink
With the quickness of the glance
Does not give you a chance

This look raising the tensions
Reveals a sense of deep connection
More than just feed the troll
Bring forth the caress of the soul

It is far from the peripheral aspect
And distant of the stare long concept
Will not bring fear like the leer
Nor the contemptuous sneer

Pardon the expression
This by the looker-on
In the eyes of the beholders
Is unlike the discomfort of the gazer

Obviously close to ogling
It gets to have that intimate meaning
Engaged in arousing feelings
Involving people interested in relating

A look can open a psychic window
Taking you out of limbo
And with this mental picture
Leave a signature

Something to get you in cohesion
Have you in obsession
The visual touch of a moment hallmarked
Like a spark

Loving eyes

cPrimping and preening for about an hour
Standing in front of the mirror
Looking at the reflection of the iris
I felt as induced in hypnosis

Perhaps I ventured beyond the mind
Leaving the brain behind
Images passing through the lens
All being cleansed

Time to be with the stars aligned
However, all was there on the pupil line
The picture-perfect of a replica
Lights bouncing off the cornea

Taking meaning by the optic gland
To where it is understood by the stand
The interpretation into a form of interest
What the nervous system is to attest

This visual organ is of the gift of sight
To things that are more than black and white
Squinting when things are arduous to see
Blinking with coquetry

Sometime will present a gawk of rudeness
As a leer of wittinessb
A display of friendly pretext
An expression that is dishonest

These eyes window to the soul
Exhibit confidence as I take on audacious roles
Will contract some tensions
On a peripheral glance evading connection

I would be lacking stimulus without them
Be regarded as blind man
Unable to enjoy the colors all around
Living mostly by touch and sound

Difficult to ogle at a woman's charismatic smile
Though I can smell her from a mile
As my prime contact the world outside
Often leaves me wide eyed

These visual senses allow me to appreciate
Mother Nature's deeds
Still attempt to make me take this as read
That beauty is only external
As I look up on them as more than miracles

A media affair

Turned on by the flicks on the monitor
I was captured by the motion pictures
Had an affair with the media
A relation with the cinema

In front of the silver screen
Taken by advertisements
I first got involved with sitcoms
Secretly going back for reruns

My days were scheduled by a "TV guide"
I was cheating on life
Awaiting for the tabloid reviews
Excited about the exhibition of the previews

In the convenience of movies on demand
I was easily bedazzled by the stardoms
Going through rentals
As if being controlled by remote

My living in this soap opera
Was the acting of a Melodrama
I will envision being a "Hollywood" superstar
As I watch those "DVDs" in high-def sound

The montage of these performing characters
Featuring indiscretions in "3D" factors
Had a special effect on my psyche
I was rated "PG-13" in live setting

Being so attentive to the composition of those script
Altered my interaction with human being
In ways that the entertainment industries enhanced
To diverse me from the reality of existence

So I had to interrupt these current programming
To go rediscover myself far from these films
In my mind clip off those make-believes
And get my focus channeled to true story

Slowly I managed to direct the thriving of my dreams
Take a lead on the events in production
Having the documentary of these scenes
Be recorded by a cast of family and friends

My day off

Sometimes as I get off the ride
Step down the routine of life
I find it hard to unwind
Let myself calm down

I think about the laboring days
As the schedule ends
And no one comes to greet me at the station
No welcoming wagon

Like being laid off from existence
With the silence that becomes
I feel vacant inside
See nothing of color beyond my eyes

My thoughts are of many shades of gray
And my dreams are fading away
There is nobody abode to goad me
Not even share a debate with me

I get to have no pillow fights
No intimate good nights
No makeup sex
Or worry about putting down the seat of the toilet

I can run around naked
Change my bedsheet once every two weeks
At my table no one to split my meal with
And I do not get anxious about washing the dishes

Is this world really my home
Or is it just a shelter from the storm
Where I pretend to be fond
Until death comes along

Through the years I have been dismissed
"Giving the boot" for my lack of living
Did I get fired for not having a soul
Or should I just continue being alone
I do not know

My Pain

I was conceived while blood shed
And there goes my fate
As proof of liveliness I had to be slapped
Cry vital sound portend I was alive

Being born with epilepsy
Was the beginning of my agony
Already I was damned
Pain was my addiction

My physical activities got retained
Making me feeling a bit lame
Bitterness got transfused into my vein
And grief became my medicine

I was hooked on basic resentments
Wanting to enjoy the rudimentary experiences
As trepidation kept my heart pulsate
The seizures got me disoriented

My hatred of the world was growing strong
I did not know where I belonged
Nor was my self-confidence enough
To accept my mental illness

Using ache as a kick
I could not help being sick
And climbing the walls of shame
Each episode had pieces of my memory scram

Hardly remembering some of the things
I have learned I felt as being left behind
And reluctant to reveal to the school my disorder
My absences were not considered of health matters

I did not want to join any special program
Afraid they will think of me as a retard
Stuff me with prescription pills
So I became an insolent guy

Sorrow was my fix
I needed to score in the big league
Continuously I listen to songs of blues
To keep me gloom

My destituteness of feeling had me panic
Turning me into a cynic
Thinking I am abnormal
Therefore becoming unsociable

Poesy

Poets are to the extreme
They go beyond the obvious feelings
Through a diction
Expressing passions and perceptions

Those emotions sometimes come through in rhythm
and rhymes Lines of harmonious designs

Poets break reality's fences
Initiating reactions that touch the senses
Convey their opinions with enthuse
Ideas introduced by a muse

Their vision of divine romance
Narrate behaviors that have significance were logic faints

Poets are of the spirits
In their verses live their magic
They can picture the soul better than any digital camera
Contribute to the wisdom of "Athena"

Their acumens can affect your morals
Have you think deep about your life's goal

Poets can bring forth popular adages
Motivate the drudge to unshackle society's elicits bondages
In a theme induced a quest
A search for justice and rightfulness

A poet can inspire the visualization of solutions
in improbable situations
Through the power of imagination
His words can evoke emancipation
Open the mind of a new generation

Precipitation

I started to snivel
Before it drizzled
Tears dropped from a serene sky
Touching everything on sight

The build up damp in the weather
That comes to weigh in the air
And slowly rises with the wet grass
Invades the surrounding areas

The Pitter-Patter of the precipitation
Was as loud as a celebration
But it was not raining frogs
Nor cats and dogs

Like a live recital on the roof set
Bewailed in merriment as a fete
This was an easygoing refrain we all recognized
But none of us could imitate with our mouths

They were notes of a unique feat
Traditionally performed in a rite's
A harmony orchestrated in taps
Spreading over the shingled tops

This shower with its thunder-storm
Had the clouds bucketing down
Pouring in heavy globules
With the wind as background chorus

Water flowing on the slanted tiles
Gathered in a dash to the gutter lines
Straight down in a dive
Rambling in descent the drainpipes

A flood on the pavement corners
Rushes the street trash to the sewers
Elevating the level of the bay
As it washes our sins away

Ray of love

Much like a ray of sunshine
Part of the grand design
Love in harmony with nature
Gives distinction to the lineament of a feature

Like the energy in the "Feng Shui" that flows
The contour of a silhouette that glows
In the nuance of obscurity it illuminates
Dazzling shades of colors are animated

It will cast the umbra aside
For the propagation of sparkling lights
To revel in the growth of life
Becoming vividly bright

It brings to a character's attraction
A reflective aura of radiance
And in a creature's appearance
The beauty of existence

In the spectrum of the eyes it glitter
Revealing the sunny side of a figure
The expression in charm
The deep sensation of warmth

Whenever it hits you in a spotlight
You will feel as though you are temporarily blind
And standing there paralyzed
All your shadows seem to fall behind

Reflection

As I meditated about the life I led
Reminiscing of what I have been handed
I found plans that did not pass my door
Dreams that are still on the shore

All of an existence kept at bay
Because of being afraid

Many doubts made me hang back
Preventing me to step out
Creating a vagueness in my living
That can only be explained in a feeling

The waves continuously rush to the coastline
Bringing unfulfilled thoughts to my mind

Somehow my fate rests on a pier
For I did not have the guts to face my fears
Scared of dealing with the high tides
The notion of the boat going down

That is why I still linger on the dock
Waiting at the marina to be rescheduled to board

Just walking around the harbor
Thinking of the successful waters
Hoping my trip will be recalled
So I can go navigate the distant ports

Regrets are all that are left on the quay
And that is my price to pay

This ship has already sailed
And this passenger has been withheld
Anchored to the idea of traveling on a departed cruiser
With a ticket That by now has expired

It is time I forget about missed opportunities
And embark on a new journey

My sentence

I had no excuses for my emotions
No justifications for being taken
My involvement was not of a premeditated act
But unfortunately, I got aroused

I attempted to fight my senses
But they had me pinned down in a trance
I was compelled to this affront
Tied up to the enticements

Useless was my practice of indifference
I could not ignore the magnetism
And like the strike of a knife
It wounded all inferences in my mind

Partly I am guilty as charged
Even if I did not instigate the advances
My response out of foolish admiration
Intentionally linked me to this crime of passion

There were many witnesses to this romance
But their statements did not assert my innocence
It only avowed perjury under oath
After I swore never to have any such interest on the bible

Although evidences of this inquiry
Were not proofs of a first degree
With no alibi explaining the presence of this fond
The jury did not care for my argument

As an entreaty to my human rights
The verdict was based on the heart
And the judge above all suspicions concluded
A ruling of meant to be

This conviction from the court of love
Is a sentence till death do us part
And with no chance for parole to come
I will cherish every conjugated session

A shy morning

It was a temperate morning
In a discrete awakening
As there began a change in the feel
And the night stars moseyed on down the hills
Retiring to the outer realm
Left the alps overwhelmed

Going through trees in the surrounded terrain
The spotlight on the mountains
With shadows hanging back on the land
As if being pushed by hand
Had a timid sun concealed in the horizon
Unveil a diffident dawn

Slowly stretched flat on the naked ground
Shades on higher mounds
Draw out behind the peak of mounts
Appearing to have the world held to account
At first light frighten and shy
Watching the golden eye rise in the sky

Distant in dreary yellow
In the mist where the cockcrow
Trying to move the needle from pointing north
Day break was hesitant to come forth
To alter the moist in the atmosphere
Make thing warm and clear

He was reluctant to let bright appeared in loom
But it was time for nature to resume
The animals to change tune
So, sunrise can proceed to noon
And in such singing mood
Have the bashful blue renewed

Therefore, he had to get rid of yesterday's mares
Induced fresh scent in the air
Rendering us to be aware of all the flowers blossoming
That comes to make up this setting

Now….. This is fit for outing
With the lively colors in the surrounding
That adorned this ragged panorama
Are to herald today's pleasant and beautiful Nirvana

Six feet under

When I go six feet under
Do not cry for this glorious bastard
Shed only tears of joy
At my obsequy just rejoice

Since I was born out of wedlock
Forget this loss tot
Leave me with my foul qualities
To rot at the coroner's office

Let this cadaver grow its molds
So it can properly decompose
Or out of respect for my spirit
Shred my body to pieces

Come to my wake dressed vividly bright
With your condolences ridiculing my demise
And bring your laughter's to my funeral
Having a festival for my memorial

After I have "bought the farm"
Burn my bones in the crematorium
Dust me out in the prairie
So I can go "pushing up daisies"

It is nothing to mourn nor grieved over
Save your prayers
No need of a eulogy for this hoodwinker
No more dealing with this joker

As I "kick the bucket"
Keep your forgiveness to yourselves
But do not hold back the insults
Knowing that I broke your hearts

Be ready to throw in the blames
With no fear of shamming my name
Go ahead and roast this deceased
Hindering me to rest in peace

Before closing the casket
Spit on my corpse as you make the sign of the cross
Put nails in my coffin
So eternally I will remain in pain

You should not cushion my space
Let me roll in my grave
For I will not appear in your séances
Until my tomb is raid in contempt

Forget about playing the requiem
Making the pipe organ solemn
And no singing the "Amazing grace"
To help me move to a better place

Put intone no religious stanza
Not even an "Ave Maria"
For my story was the tale of an idiot
The epic of a mote

My departure was a blow
A waste of life with no sweet sorrows
I was but the demon living among you
A walking dead that time has finally eluted

Smart play

You want to play it smart
A chance for a new start
Stop throwing darts
For you are willing to take a shot
Get a "bull's eye"

Tired of the game of hardball
Feelings like you never have a goal
You yearn for a strike
Add point to your chart
And score for life

Since you have met your match
You have been marked
Someone hit you in the right spot
Therefore as a major target
You are becoming a great catch

Now in the big leagues
With your name on the billboard
No longer on the side line
Your every move will be a counteract
On how you are being Challenged on the courtyard

Overtaking such stake
Makes you the ideal teammate
And trusting your instinct
With the body language you present
Demonstrate a certain talent

For when the calling hence
And gently you let off your defense
Stepping into forward position
As things are kicked in the open
Will secure you a "home run"

Although what you have can be of a steal
One has to be focused on the field
Do more than receiving
As well as learning to seize the moment
To deliver a "touch down"

While engaged in this sport
You have tackled the heart
Take things beyond physical contact
And with such a deserving winning
Bless there be a "brass ring"

The Special

When the reality served
Gets to be better than the dream you ordered
Something is to be particular

You can smell the passion in the air
The sultriness in the atmosphere
That arouses the senses and tenses the nerves

Therefore do not go filling on "hors d'oeuvre"
Be cordial to your caterer
Let it be love that comes to wait on the table

You are privileged to the chef's special
Selection of the exceptional
That sizzles your appetite

Prepared in "Culinary art"
This that seasoned your thoughts
Will spice your heart

It does not have to be of a "Royal Feast"
But will flavor the best life has to offer
For you are worthy of such honor

Be thankful of this "Cordon Bleu" dinner
It is not like the "fast-food" drive-through "take out"
Nor the call delivery "drop out"

This is cuisine delicacy
So do not sour your fate
Eat no more than what is in your plate

If you want to add zest to your sate
Just a heartfelt touch will get it to stimulate
And you will savor the taste

The Subway artist

To the subway artist
Life seems to be of malice
On the train tunnel day after day
He carries on with no certainty of pay

Performing his act
Always improving on his knack
He makes his living on sound
Joining the clang of the rails downtown

At the station Strumming his guitar
He often takes on a phonic ride the crowd
Brings the commuters some sort of satisfaction
With his tuneful expressions

His goal has an artisan
He's not about making record platinum
And even if not getting too much consideration
He does not feel betrayed by his passion

He is a token of enthusiasm
A one-man band
Enjoys his time on the underground line
Where the echo of the music transit the musician

Taking into account

Even in the climate of civilization
Man has yet to achieve gumption
Constituting self-worth to be of income
Forgetting nothing is to equal the price of wisdom
With it a greed for acquisitions
As he remains obsessed with possessions

The geniuses in refining being human
Executing their strategic plan
Put aside the old principles of the sages
To go take the moral wages
That we should in status
Be appraised on economical values

Every day it gets harder to be decent
Little by little, we are out of the element
Caught only thinking of the sum and substance
Seemingly losing our conscience
As integrity becomes sordid
While unscrupulous acts are being rewarded

On our constant trivial mindedness
We slowly move into pettiness
Having our friends turned into liabilities
As we misplaced our sense of magnanimity
Becoming no more than material assets
We tend to be morally bankrupt

With only a yearn for dominance
Our merits based on finance
We'll go the whole nine yard
Of getting to be about plastic cards
The glory that blessing anoint
To practically become credit points

It all being capitalized
Playing stupid games and wining stupid prize
By practice a note on debit
This modernization destroys our natural benefits
Have us become accustomed to hearing interest accrued
Balance due

Talking

There is a beauty in a sound
And art in the words pronounced
That can inspire a crowd
Or allows the truth to come out

As you think out loud
Let the articulation rise
Have your tone be upbeat
But do not let it come like a trumpet

In the time of verbal language
Making a tongue phrase
Take part in the argument
With no lip-giving

Showing your gift of gab
Can also be of a prep talk
And something mentioned in the chatterbox
Does not have to be like a "wolf ticket"

Have your speech be positive
Express something deep
Define your inner feelings
Without the rush of passing judgments

Do not go playing the meanings
Changing the clauses representations
Using the tact of a politician
To get favors for your cant

Open your mouth
And speak your mind
Be ready to make your statement
Not a sermon

Discourse clearly your reasons
But do not flap your gum
Address any disagreements
Make a comment

Has there been an informative prologue
That flows into a dialogue
Exchange the ideas
In a communication among peers

Make no different what is your lingo
The dictionary should be your friend
Let it help you engage a conversation
Voice your honest opinions

Third degree

Being of the inner city
Got me confined as if by a decree
Like having an ankle bracelet
Put on house arrest

Becoming socially dreaded
Feeling like a jailbird
With my interests tethered
To the harsh existence in the project

According to public hearing
Already I was guilty
And in the regard of my wretched style
I was to be an obscene child

Being restricted by the bourgeoisie
And always getting the third degree
With hand over my head
I was hitting the deck

Living on my knees
With everything I say being used against me
Even in the court of law
I was being mauled

Unable to afford my dream
I assumed the position
And got caught exploited by the administrations
With no way of bailing out the daily treatments

I thought it was a trial run
Keeping me from lying down on the pavement
But this weekly earning
Had me ignoring my calling

In a separate but equal judgment
I took the settlement
And beyond reasonable doubts
Made it my life

To the hand

I was shown the palm
Was told to talk to the hand
It stretches like the sign of a high-five
But that was not what it symbolized

It was that I should stop speaking
Because the ears were not listening
And as she turned her face aside
Her iris rolled up to hide behind her lashes

I kept at loud my speech
For she could not have me mute
She heeded every word I cursed
But pretended she was deaf

Playing hard of hearing
And never engaging the argument
Ignoring what I was saying
In an expression of silent miff

To the end as a rhetorical answer
I was given the middle finger
A gesture with a sudden grunt
That felt like an onslaught

My thoughts were inflamed
Upon receiving this flip
As she pointed out adding with a last shout
That I should stick it where the sun does not shine

A tone

There is a melody to a hum
A grunt in every man
A tempo distinctive to his life
A tune that he chimes

There is an accent when he talks
An imprint in his voice
A rhythm when he sighs
A pulse in his heart

He is part of the grand symphony orchestra
The leading libretto in this opera
In his absence the notes are not synchronized
Making this philharmonic destitute in rhyme

He has a unique role in this worldly composition
The highs and lows are special for his function
They are the writing of a classical
Eminent characters to this musical

His performance as a vocalist
Makes this renowned choir what it is
Through the years he has gathered his theatrical repertoire
Singing his ensemble in this conservatoire

Une autre histoire d' Haiti
(Another story of Haiti)

Panic was what it brought
On the Westside of the island of "Hispagniola"
It came without warning
Adding to the famine

At a measure of seven point zero
Devastation elevated the death toll
In the course of heavy turbulence
Crumpling the city of "Port-au-Prince"

Nature was in a rage
"Rant and rave" a rampage
Abruptly heaving the establishments
Destroying lifetime achievements

Leaving the public empty-handed
With only agony to salvage
As a stream of red blood on the ground
Under the blue Caribbean sky met to reflect the Haitian flag

This sudden strike of havoc
Had children trapped under feet of rocks
Voicing the tumult of desolation
In this site of living damnation

Some of the thousands who got injured
As they tried to walk the wreck
Went above and beyond
Facing the situation by giving a hand

Surviving with more than a will
Those few "Boukmans" with no means or skills
Reached out to rescue their peasant brothers
As grace under pressure

It was a major force of human behaviors
That upstaged those laborers
From being more than just victims of a quake
To brave Meeks

For this award-winning performance
In this Creole terrain
January 12th could also be regarded as a day of heroism
For this might have made shiver the tropical sun

This quivering dread
Has put neighborhoods into shred
In an attempt to increase drama in the country
Augment the meager look of the communities

Taking away of next of kin
Have traumatized many families
But the compassion of many other nations
Helped the people mourn those unforgotten

As another chapter of Haitian history
This was a coup of no political parties
There were no factions and no partisans
No one had adherence to any allegiances

The "Tonton Makouts" were not there to crash
the rebellious freedom fighters
It was a struggle for survival against nature
On one of the world's poorest capital
Leaving the deceased in the heat to dry

Through these seismic activities that hope had to claim
This chaos unlike "Katrina" had no name
So they could not curse it out
Nor put voodoo spell on its mayhem

It kept on testing the strength of the wounded
The faith in the spirited
The heart of those who lost a loved one
And the courage in those whose dreams have been crushed

To wave its turmoil
It smeared colors on the soil
As it walked about
Leaving its ruins to make up the town

Reminding the "Negre Maron" (running slave)
As it horns his conch
That even after the rainfall washes the stain clean
The splotch memory of this tragedy will forever be

Urban tabloid

She was the paparazzi of the lower class
The tabloid of the mass
Getting in everybody's businesses
Snooping like the daily news

The first to shout out any indiscretions
Detailing all transgressions
This cheeky raconteur in her gossips
Brings to the public your story

She will be prying into your affairs
Blab the recent events into the air
Updating the rumors about your life
Have your imprudence advertised

Unofficially the local reporter
As if taking from a teleprompter
In her unregulated programming
On live stream media broadcasting

She will yap about your indignities
Making a propaganda of your fetishes
Buzzed these audio transmissions
In the convenience of a 7-eleven operation

She will tittle-tattle your outrages
Gives you a bad name
At no time holding anything back
A meter mouth

Similar to the internet chat
She longs to talk on the party line
Is the voice that never stops
The barking that wakes the neighbors up

Her urban bulletin scandals
Are the records of indecent proposals
That rattled the privacy act
Playing on like a scratched soundtrack

Always keeping her ears open
Lip serving all day long
With her around the skeletons are crawling out of the closets
Every single subject is of her interest

A vagabond

I was a bum
Part of the slum
Just there to pick up the crumbs
Stick like a sore thump
Was treated as but another vagabond

Spat out like a piece of gum
And stepped on like an extraneous scrap on the pavement
Something being dragged along a shoe bottom
I was considered to be nothing but an earth scum
A filthy slim

I had no saving fun
Led the life of a humdrum
Waiting to be summoned
Therefore a chump
Who was always glum

My opinions were never conferred in the forum
For already they wrote my future in the memorandum
And according to society's dictum
I would by no means swim out of the swamp
In no way get to sit in the sun

Thus contrary to what they assumed
I heeded the whisper of a different hum
My heart beats were of a particular tom-tom
A sound of a distinct rhythm
Making me feel as singing a song

I started to string a strum
Having my poetry rhyme
As if carving my own totem
While holding destiny in my palm
And I was not about to throw it in the dump

Vibe

In the unusual rhythm of life
I caught a quiver up my spine
Struck by an electrical discharge
That blew my mind

Suddenly feeling that vibe
Cheek to cheek with love
I was dancing "a pas de deux"
Grinding in a quixotic manner

Involved in an old-fashioned cadence
Of a slow romance
I was aware of the texture of her palms
Sensing the blood that flows through her hands

It was like being in the metamorphosis
A step on rainbow bliss
Transmutation into higher bound
Beyond the physical form

Over and above the crowd
Boogied on surrounded by stars
I was moonwalking the silver line
Floating on cloud nine

In this ballroom in the sky
I started to glide
Moving to the pulse of a waltz
For this was more than a bop

Vintage

Such as fine wine
Women are the elixir of life
The brew that attenuates the mind
The poison that inflames the heart

They can have you think you are drinking from the grail
Get you more inebriated than any ale
And in their fermented high-degree seduction
Have you affected as if by a love potion

Of a sophisticated bearing stance
And a smile that savor the silence
They capture the eyes of the aficionados
With desirable traits deem to the pharaohs

As the outcome of heaven and earth
There is no merit to what they are worth
And in the gracefulness of body languages
They can bring saccharine urges

Women are the essence of what it is to be debonair
The obsession of all connoisseurs
They rapt the romantic sites
Embraced the erotic nights

They are irresistible in their delicate shells
Quite subtle as damsels
They can fill you with daily awes
Or suddenly make you wow

Women with their eloquence
are at a vantage point
And with their prestigious "femme fatale" personas
Seize the marvel of a diva

Women of an Epiphany Through Time
Are the vintage of mankind
Most luscious among all creatures under the sky
The eternal thirst of the "Greek Gods"

A garden Weed

Be it ever so humble
Grasping the nettle
A weed is legendary
Living by its own philosophy
Knows about rough terrain
Does not wait in disdain

A weed in its strife
Is high on life
Passionate and full of pride
It can appear through hanging on a crack in the wall
Living on the wild side
Or spotted on the pavement standing tall

A weed for not born of privilege
As yet to be acknowledged
Doesn't deem necessary to have tillage
Needs no gardening to help it manage
Growing where it's not wanted
Making it home not to be persecuted

Famous for its stalk and slender reed
Going around spreading its seeds
Way beyond its means
Just green that blends with the grass
Strong enough to hang along the edge of a fen
Or a breed trying to mingle with the mass

A weed has been inclined
To be a flower unrefined
Able to dwell on a soil uncultivated
It is a shrub not yet appreciated
Knows nothing about tender loving care
No one never taught it how to share

A weed is a plant not yet loved
Troublesome to get rid of
But it is comfortable to be mowed away
Knowing it will never be Part of a bouquet
nor mixed with Potpourri

Wild Thing

Can man be domesticated
Can he be outside a social cage
And live without a tag

Can he get along with his neighbors cats
Share his milk-bones with a pal
And avoid barking for a fight

Can he as a mutt from the kennel
Restrain from digging holes in the backyard
And not bring his filth inside the house

Is it too hard for him to find an alternate means of hygiene
Other than using his tongue
Licking himself clean

Can he stop jumping the fence
To go humping at everything in sight
And quit sniffing buttocks

Can he stick to his peeing on fire-hydrant routine
Stop urinating on the carpeting
And cease his toilet-bowl drinking

Can he stop chasing his own hind
And while wiggling his tail with excitements
Not bite the hand that feeds him

Can he as a pit-bull on guard
Stop being a wild card
And limit his flea act to the junkyard

Can he come when called
Go fetch a ball
And halt on the growl

After being house-broken
Will he be potty trained
Learn to leave his excrements in the litter pan

Can he run without the leash of the law
Playing tricks on two paws
Make human rights a standard for all